American adaptation copyright © 2013 by NorthSouth Books Inc., New York 10016.
Copyright © 2013 by NordSüd Verlag AG, CH-8005 Zürich, Switzerland.
First published in Switzerland under the title *Mein kunterbuntes Tier-ABC.*
English translation copyright © 2013 by NorthSouth Books Inc., New York 10016.
Designed by Pamela Darcy of Neo9 Design Inc.

First published in the United States, Great Britain, Canada, Australia, and
New Zealand in 2013 by NorthSouth Books Inc., an imprint of NordSüd
Verlag AG, CH-8005 Zürich, Switzerland.

Distributed in the United States by NorthSouth Books Inc., New York 10016.
Library of Congress Cataloging-in-Publication Data is available.
ISBN: 978-0-7358-4136-9
Printed in Germany by Offizin Andersen Nexö Leipzig GmbH, 04442 Zwenkau, November 2013.
3 5 7 9 • 10 8 6 4 2
www.northsouth.com
Meet Marcus Pfister at www.marcuspfister.ch

FSC
www.fsc.org
MIX
Aus verantwortungs-
vollen Quellen
FSC® C043106

Marcus Pfister

Animal
ABC

North
South

A a

I have scales and a toothy smile.
Just don't call me "crocodile."

Alligator

My cozy fur is thick and brown.
If I smell honey, I'll come around.

Bear

Cc

I can blend in with a leaf or a tree,
Changing my colors so you can't see me.

Chameleon

Dd

I swim like a fish but breathe in air.
I can do flips and jumps with flair.

Dolphin

Ee

I use my trunk to drink and eat.
I walk around on soft, round feet.

Elephant

Ff

I hop around and eat with my tongue.
I was a tadpole when I was young.

Frog

Gg

My spotted neck can reach the sky.
I like to watch the birds fly by.

Giraffe

Hh

I have long ears and I look like a bunny,
But I'm much faster. Isn't that funny?

Hare

Ii

I'm a lizard with really good eyes.
I can see so far, it's quite a surprise.

Iguana

J j

I'm a big cat that likes to swim.
I can climb a tree and sit on its limb.

Jaguar

Kk

I carry my baby in a pouch.
I might look slow, but I'm no slouch.

Kangaroo

King of the jungle—look at me.
I'm very loud but quite lazy!

Lion

Mm

Into tiny places I can squeeze,
Especially if I smell some cheese!

Mouse

Nn

I'm like an anteater but not quite!
I don't eat ants—I eat termites.

Numbat

I'm a smart ape; I live in the trees.
I eat healthy fruit, if you please.

Orangutan

P p

I'm a bird that cannot fly,
But I can swim. Don't ask me why.

Penguin

Qq

I'm brightly colored as you can see,
But I'm hard to spot when I'm in a tree.

Quetzal

Rr

I can dive and roll in the sky
And be upside down when I fly.

Raven

Ss

I can toot a horn or balance a ball,
But eating a fish is my best trick of all.

Sea Lion

Tt

I'm the biggest cat and have great sight.
I like to hunt for food at night.

Tiger

Uu

I'm a horse with a spiral horn.
In someone's dream I was born.

Unicorn

V v

I'm a snake with a poisonous bite.
My venom protects me in a fight.

Viper

W w

I have a small pouch, like a kangaroo.
I live in Australia and the zoo.

Wombat

Made-up creatures are so much fun.
Give it a try! Can you make one?

Xylophonius

Yy

I'm like a cow, but I have long hair.
My wool is used for things to wear.

Yak

I have stripes and I look like a horse,
But my name begins with "z," of course!

Zebra

Other books by Marcus Pfister . . .

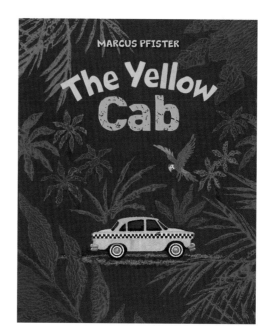